KICKSTART

WARD 6

CREATED AND WRITTEN BY
KEVIN FOX

ART BY
SALVADOR NAVARRO

COVER BY
NORBERTO FERNANDEZ

COLORS BY
ALEJANDRO SANCHEZ RODRIGUEZ
& DAVID HUESO

LETTERS & DESIGN BY
BILL TORTOLINI
PRODUCED BY
KICKSTART COMICS

 For Kickstart Comics Inc:
Samantha Shear, Managing Editor

THESE ARE
THEIR ASSIGNMENTS.
DO WHAT YOU WANT,
AS LONG AS THEY
KEEP SOLVING
PROBLEMS FOR
US.

THE INSTITUTE,
ADMINISTRATION BUILDING

THE LIBRARY —AFTER

SARA D'ORLEANS, CANONIZED 1923. FIVE MIRACLES ATTRIBUTED TO HER. WE'RE ALL HERE, LEO...

LEON PETROVICH, ONCE CONSIDERED HEIR TO STALIN. PETROVICH CARRIED OUT MOST OF THE 20 MILLION DEATHS STALIN ORDERED.

NO. THAT CAN'T BE RIGHT.

ME...NICOLE GRIZEL, AN INVENTOR. MAJOR CONTRIBUTOR TO THE BIRTH OF MODERN COMPUTING... DISAPPEARED IN MARCH OF 1982.

SEAN CONNELLY, A LEADER OF THE IRA, KILLED IN 1922 BY MEN LOYAL TO EAMON DEVALERA...

CATRIONA NOLAN, A NURSE, WAS SEAN CONNELLY'S FIANCÉ.

WHAT DID YOU FIND?

I FOUND OUT WHO WE ARE.

SARA – YOU NEED TO START PRAYING MORE, WANDERING THE WOODS.

...TO LEAVE A BLOOD TRAIL.

LEO, WE'LL NEED TO GET YOU SOME KIND OF WEAPON.

THEN WE NEED TO IDENTIFY OUR ENEMIES. FIND EVIDENCE TO FIND THEM OUTSIDE THESE WALLS...

THE LIBRARY - LATER

DOCTOR CARLSON YANG. DEPUTY DIRECTOR AND SPECIAL GOVERNMENT ADVISER TO DOCTOR SOPHIA PRIMO'S RESEARCH LABS.

GO! DON'T STOP--

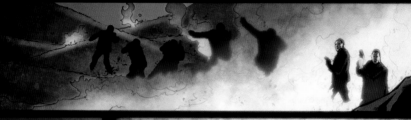

...SO ALIX WAS THE FIRST TO SACRIFICE HERSELF.

WHOOM

WE HAD IT ALL PLANNED OUT. A SCORCHED EARTH POLICY. NOTHING OF US, OR THEM, LEFT BEHIND...

KRRRUMMMBLE

THERE WAS ONLY ONE
WAY TO MAKE SURE
OF THAT..

WE NEEDED TO MAKE
SURE THEY NEVER
CHASED US...

NEVER KNEW THAT WE WERE
STILL ALIVE TO CHASE.

WE NEEDED
TO DIE.

Divine Wind

WRITTEN BY JEFF Y. AMANO

HAKATA BAY. JAPAN.

"The other day, a boy cut off the head of a snake. His parents cried out to me, wanting to know if their son committed a karmic transgression."

"I told them to reward their son with a sweet bean cake."

"Had the snake entered my temple, it would be well-cared for. Had the snake remained in the forest, he would enjoy the bounty of the wild. But it ventured into the boy's home and paid the price of trespass."

"That is the Way of things."

"Across the Sea of Japan..."

"... a swarm of serpents have slithered through China, knowing no boundaries,..."

"... knowing no equal. In addition to land and treasures, they acquire the warriors and weaponry of their conquered, creating the largest military force on Earth."

"But it was not enough for Kublai Khan, Lord of the Mongols."

Divine Wind

WRITTEN BY JEFF Y. AMANO

"Not nearly enough."

And yet an island of warring natives have refused to pay me tribute.

There is no head in all Mongolia, Korea, and Northern China that does not bow to your shadow. Soon Southern China will fall and all Asia will be yours.

"Then the desert snake set his sights on our island."

... but General Arakhan, surely you realize that our armies are stretched to the limit from the war with Southern China.

And we're so close to victory. We promised our troops a reprieve...

Mongols know no "reprieve." Without war, we are sheep in wolves' clothing.

"Kublai Khan sent 900 ships and 30,000 troops to Japan,..."

"... but 4,000 samurai drove the Mongols back into the maw of the sea dragon."

WRITTEN BY MATT MAIELLARO

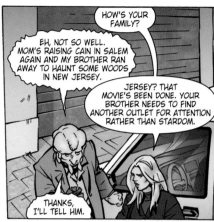

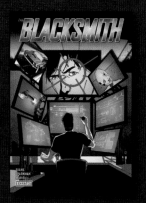

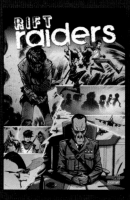